written by Henrietta D. Gambill

illustrated by Joe Boddy

Library of Congress Catalog Card Number 89-52031

"Little lamb," David said, "you've got to stop running off from the flock. I had to save you again today. That lion had you in its mouth. He was getting ready to eat you up."

The lamb nestled in David's arms as David talked softly to it. And it felt safe with David, the shepherd boy.

"I'm leaving now to go visit my brothers in the army of Israel. They are fighting the Philistines. My father wants me to take food to them.

"Now you must stay near Jethro while I'm gone. He's the shepherd who will take care of you."

David put the little lamb down and picked up the bundle of food. But as he walked away, the lamb started to follow him.

"No, no," David said. "You can't go with me. Now run on back to Jethro."

The lamb stopped and looked back at Jethro as David walked hurriedly away. David wanted to get to the battle. He wondered how his brothers and the Israelite army were doing. He wanted to know if they were winning.

David enjoyed going to the army camp. It was always exciting to see a battle. David wished he could be in the army of Israel, but he couldn't. He was much too young. *But I'm not afraid to fight in the army,* he thought. *God is with us because we are His special people.*

That day as he neared the army camp, David noticed something was wrong. The soldiers of Israel were preparing for battle, but David could tell they were afraid.

Just then a loud voice boomed across the valley, "You Israelites are a bunch of cowards! None of you will fight me!"

David looked up and there on a nearby hill stood the biggest man he had ever seen—a giant almost ten feet tall!

This giant named Goliath was covered with armor. His whole body was in a metal covering. And in front of the giant was a big shield carried by a soldier.

David asked about the giant, "Why won't anyone fight this man Goliath?"

"Because no one in our army is brave enough," they answered. "Goliath will kill anyone who fights him. Just look how big and strong he is. But if someone would fight him, the battle would be over."

David watched Goliath strutting back and forth. Then he said, "I will fight this Philistine. I'm not afraid of him. God will help me."

The soldiers just looked at David. He was only a boy. He couldn't fight Goliath. What was the matter with David anyway?

They hurried to tell his older brother, Eliab, what David had said. "Your little brother David is planning to fight Goliath. He'll be killed!"

This news made Eliab very angry with David. How could his little brother fight a giant! Eliab thought David was just showing off.

"You are bragging, David!" Eliab shouted at him. "You should go home and care for the sheep. You're not big enough to fight anyone!"

But one of the soldiers told King Saul what David had said. And the king was happy to hear that David wanted to fight the giant.

"If David will fight Goliath, I'll give him my armor to wear. He can have my sword to use too. Bring him to me at once."

When David was dressed in Saul's armor, he could hardy move, much less walk.

"No, no," David said. "I don't need all of this armor to cover me. I'm not used to wearing these things. Just let me go as I am, in my shepherd's clothes. God will take care of me. He has often helped me kill lions and bears when they have tried to take any sheep from my flock."

So David took off the armor and began to walk slowly toward the giant. He had only his sling to fight with.

Goliath made fun of David when he saw David coming to fight him. “Are you fighting me with just a stick? You must be crazy. I’ll kill you easily.”

Then Goliath began to curse David. But David didn't seem to notice. He just walked calmly to a stream of water. There he stooped down and chose five smooth stones. He picked just the ones he wanted and put them in a pouch.

Then David answered Goliath. "You come to fight me with a sword and spears. But I come to fight you in the name of the Lord. He will help me kill you and win the victory for Israel."

As Goliath came near, David began to run toward him. All the soldiers of Israel watched in fear as David got nearer and nearer to the giant. They couldn't believe it was really happening. And David didn't seem to be afraid at all. He just reached into his pouch and took out one of the smooth stones. He carefully put it into his sling. Then with all his strength, David flung it toward Goliath!

The stone flew through the air. Faster and faster!

It went straight for Goliath's head. The stone struck the giant in the middle of his forehead, and he immediately fell down. The ground shook as his big body fell with a loud thud. He lay without moving. The mighty giant was no longer able to get up and fight!

The soldiers stood silently watching. They couldn't believe the giant who had created such fear in them was down on the ground. It had seemed so easy for David. All he had done was fling a small, smooth stone from his sling.

Then David ran to Goliath and grabbed the giant's sword. He used it to kill Goliath.

The soldiers shouted and cheered. David was a hero! God had used him—a small shepherd boy—to kill a mighty giant.

This made the soldiers of Israel so brave, they chased after the Philistine army and won the victory that day.